BONJOUR L'ENFANT!

Acknowledgment:

To my husband, Brad, for his love and support,

and to my children, M & E, our journey continues...

Danna

AuthorHouse™
1663 Liberty Drive, Suite 200
Bloomington, IN 47403
www.authorhouse.com
Phone: 1-800-839-8640

AuthorHouse™ UK Ltd.
500 Avebury Boulevard
Central Milton Keynes, MK9 2BE
www.authorhouse.co.uk
Phone: 08001974150

Bloomington, IN   authorHOUSE™   Milton Keynes, UK

First published by AuthorHouse 10/10/2006

ISBN: 1-4259-6484-2 (sc)
ISBN: 1-4259-6521-0 (dj)

Library of Congress Control Number: 2006908354
Printed in Canada

This book is printed on acid-free paper.

www.ciaobambinobooks.com

CIAO BAMBINO!™

BONJOUR L'ENFANT!

A Child's Tour of France

BY **Danna Troncatty Leahy**

ILLUSTRATED BY **Gabhor Utomo**

the CIAO BAMBINO! book series

www.ciaobambinobooks.com

AuthorHouse Publishing

Bonjour L'Enfant!

C'est moi, Michael.

Can you guess where my

family went this summer?

Oui! – Mommy and Daddy took us to France. It was my sister Elizabeth's first trip across the big ocean. My teddy bear Globe came too. He goes everywhere I go.

Atlantic Ocean

Europe

France is the biggest country in Western Europe. It looks like a star to me, but grown-ups call it *L' Hexagone*. Do you see six sides?

Voilà!

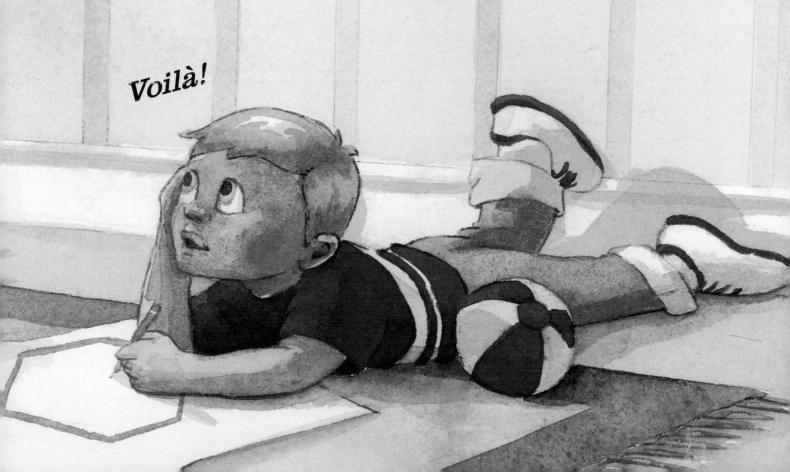

In France, they don't speak English.

They speak French.

Parlez-vous français?

Let's learn together!

Très bien! Alors commençons!

Our adventure began in Paris. We spent hours by the river bank watching artists paint pictures and play music. I danced and sang along even when I didn't know the words.

"Oh la, la. J'aime chanter et danser à Paris."

Seine River

One day we discovered the top of the world. Well, I can't imagine anything taller than the Eiffel Tower. We climbed hundreds of steps and took an elevator to the very top. Globe found his own way up.

A tout à l'heure!

Bonne chance!

Another afternoon, we watched an exciting bike race. It's called *Le Tour de France*. Bicyclists from around the world compete. They ride really far for weeks and finish on a famous street in Paris. Can you name the days of the week with me?

Dimanche Lundi Mardi Mercredi Jeudi Vendredi Samedi

FINISH

Champs Elysées

Attention! *Mona Lisa*

France has some of the greatest museums in the world. One giant museum used to be a king's palace, but now it is a gallery filled with sculptures and paintings. My favorite picture was the smiling lady whose eyes follow you. Beware! She is always watching.

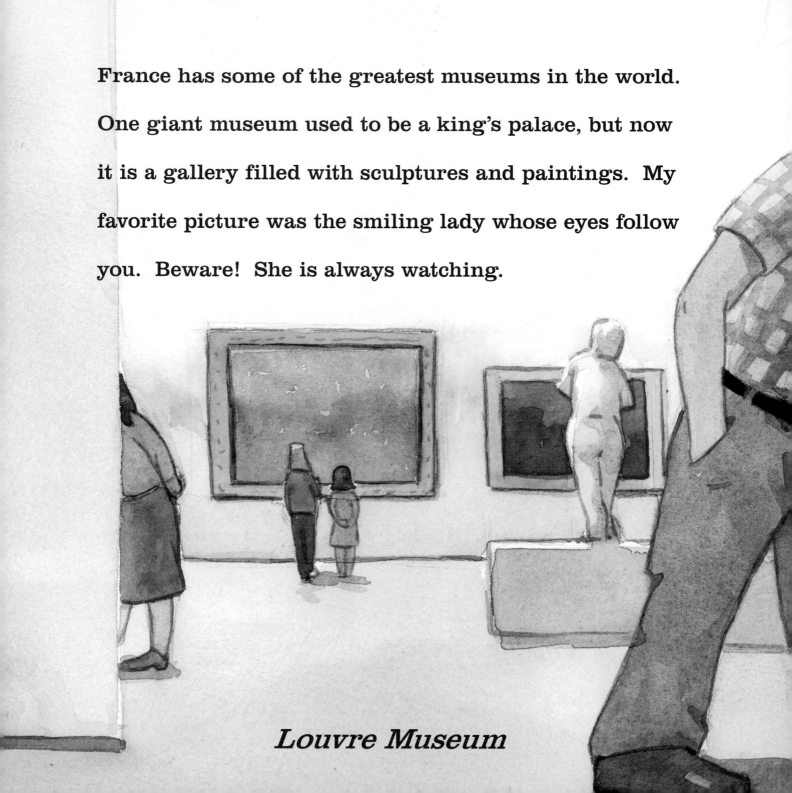

Louvre Museum

At a pretty garden outside of Paris, we learned about a man who painted pictures of water lilies. I watched the water ripple to the edge of the pond and counted the lily pads. Can you help me count to ten?

Trois

Deux

Six

Un

Cinq

Quatre

Huit

Neuf

After exploring Paris, we took a train to the valley. We visited many beautiful *châteaux*. I pretended to rule the kingdom and protect the royal princess. Our noble knight Globe guarded the castle from evil enemies.

Loire Valley

Traveling south, we toured the countryside. The fields of lavender looked like a sea of purple flowers. Our guide, Jean-Pierre, explained how the flowers are used to make fancy perfumes and soaps. Elizabeth sprayed *les parfums* everywhere, but I quickly escaped.

Provence

Our vacation ended on the sunny coast. From *la plage*, I admired the huge boats. Their colorful sails made a beautiful rainbow across the water. Let's learn the colors in French.

Bleu   Rouge   Jaune   Violet   Vert   Orange

Côte d'Azur

French food was delicious. I ate loaves of crunchy bread filled with cheese and butter. Elizabeth liked special pancakes, called *crêpes*, that were smothered in powdered sugar and jelly. Every meal was a yummy feast.

But my favorite treat was *pommes frites*, or french fries. At every restaurant I would ask *le garçon*, "*encore des pommes frites s'il vous plaît.*" When the food arrived, I'd smile and say "*merci beaucoup!*"

Mommy and Daddy said we will
go on another vacation soon.
Maybe you can go too!

Au revoir et bon voyage!

Goodbye and
good travels!

BONJOUR L'ENFANT! *Pronunciation and Translation Guide*

French Word/Phrase	Pronunciation Guide	English Translation
bonjour l'enfant	boh<u>n</u>-zhoor l'awn-faw<u>n</u>	hello child
c'est moi	say mwah	it's me
oui	wee	yes
L' Hexagone	l'ex-a-gohn	the hexagon
voilà!	vwah-lah	there it is
parlez-vous français	par-lay voo frahn-seh	do you speak French
très bien	treh bee-ah<u>n</u>	very good
alors commençons	ah-lohr koh-maw<u>n</u>-soh<u>n</u>	let's begin
oh la, la	oo lah lah	oh ah
j'aime	zhem	I love
chanter	shahn-tay	to sing
et	ay	and
danser	dahns-ay	to dance
à Paris	ah Pah-ree	in Paris
a tout à l'heure	ah too tah luhr	see you later
bonne chance	bun shahns	good luck
Dimanche	dee-mahnsh	Sunday
Lundi	lah<u>n</u>-dee	Monday
Mardi	mahr-dee	Tuesday
Mercredi	mare-kruh-dee	Wednesday
Jeudi	zhuh-dee	Thursday
Vendredi	vahn-druh-dee	Friday
Samedi	sahm-dee	Saturday
attention	ah-tahn-see-ohn	look out/be careful
un	uh<u>n</u>	one
deux	duh	two
trois	twah	three
quatre	kat	four
cinq	sank	five
six	seess	six

French Word/Phrase	Pronunciation Guide	English Translation
sept	set	seven
huit	weet	eight
neuf	nuhf	nine
dix	deess	ten
c'est bon	say boh<u>n</u>	that's good
châteaux	shah-toe	castles
vive la France!	veev lah frahns	long live France
les parfums	lay par-foom	the perfumes
allons-y	ah-lohn-zee	let's go
la plage	lah plahzh	the beach
blanc/he	bla<u>wn</u>/sh	white
bleu/e	bluh	blue
rouge	roozh	red
jaune	zhoh<u>n</u>	yellow
violet/te	vee-oh-leh/lett	purple
vert/e	vehr/t	green
orange	oh-rahnzh	orange
crêpes	krehp	pancakes
délicieux	de-lis-yuh	delicious
pommes frites	pohm freet	french fries
le garcon	luh gar-soh<u>n</u>	the waiter
encore	aw<u>n</u>-kore	more/again
s'il vous plait	seel voo pleh	please
merci beaucoup	mair-see boh-koo	thank you very much
au revoir	ohr-vwah	goodbye
bon voyage	boh<u>n</u> vwah-yaj	good travels